THIS IS A BORZOI BOOK PUBLISHED BY ALFRED A. KNOPF

Text copyright © 2013 by Aaron Reynolds
Jacket art and interior illustrations copyright © 2013 by David Barneda

Visit us on the Web! randomhouse.com/kids

Educators and librarians, for a variety of teaching tools, visit us at RHTeachersLibrarians.com

Library of Congress Cataloging-in-Publication Data
Reynolds, Aaron.
Pirates vs. cowboys / by Aaron Reynolds ; illustrated by David Barneda. — 1st ed.
p.   cm.
Summary: A scurvy pirate crew, led by Burnt Beard, finds trouble when they try to hide their treasure
in Old Cheyenne and have some miscommunication with Black Bob McKraw and his posse.
ISBN 978-0-375-85874-1 (trade) — ISBN 978-0-375-95874-8 (lib. bdg.)
[1. Interpersonal communication—Fiction. 2. Pirates—Fiction. 3. Cowboys—Fiction. 4. Humorous stories.
5. West (U.S.)—History—Fiction.] 1. Barneda, David, ill. 11. Title. 111. Title: Pirates versus cowboys.
PZ7.R33213Pir 2013
[Fic]—dc23
2012007760

The illustrations were created using acrylic paint and green horn colored pencil.

MANUFACTURED IN MALAYSIA
March 2013
10 9 8 7 6 5 4 3 2 1

First Edition

by
Aaron Reynolds

illustrated by
David Barneda

ALFRED A. KNOPF • NEW YORK

Burnt Beard the Pirate was the scourge of the seven seas, the four oceans, and several lakes.

His scurvy crew had ransacked so many ships and pillaged so many villages that all their treasure had them riding low and slow.

It was time to go ashore
and bury the booty.

Their usual spots were filled to the gills,

so those pirates went inland.

All the way to Old Cheyenne.

Black Bob McKraw was the
terror of the Wild West.

His gang of rip-roarin' rustlers
were nastier than week-old chili,
and twice as gassy.

And when they weren't out causin' mayhem on the open range, they made their roost in the town of Old Cheyenne.

So,
needless to say,
it was a sad and sorry day
when Burnt Beard the Pirate
and his crew swaggered
into Old Cheyenne.

Black Bob McKraw noticed them right away.
And that was the start of the pirate-cowboy showdown.

"Look at the duds on them scallywags," Black Bob said to his posse, which is a nasty thing to say about anyone, even if they are pirates.

To Burnt Beard's credit, he acted real civil at first, which wasn't at all in his nature.

"Ahoy there, me hearties! Be ye knowin' where we'd be findin' a fair scrub and a swish?"

Black Bob rode up real close to Burnt Beard.

"What'd you call us, ya yellow-bellied varmints?" was Black Bob's reply. "Why don't ya mangy hornswogglers beat a trail of dust right back out of Old Cheyenne!"

Burnt Beard tried again.

"Arrrgh, ye bilge rats! Be pointin' us to some grub and grog or we'll be keelhaulin' the lot o' ye!"

It didn't take them long to realize that none of them could understand one lick of what the others were saying.

None of them cowboys spoke
Pirate, and none of them
pirates spoke Cowboy!
And that's a recipe for trouble.

The more

they talked,

the madder

they got.

"Weigh anchor, ye swabs, or you'll be walkin' the plank and feedin' the fish!"

Burnt Beard snarled.
His crew grabbed for
their cutlasses.

GRRR

"You rootin'-tootin' critters better head fer the hills, or yer gonna get horsewhipped and hogtied like there's no tomorrow!"

Black Bob scoffed. His posse reached for their six-shooters.

Pistols pointed.

Swords flashed.

Lips sneered.

Nostrils flared.

Things were just about to get ugly, as pirates, cowboys, and simple misunderstandings can, when Pegleg Highnoon rode into town.

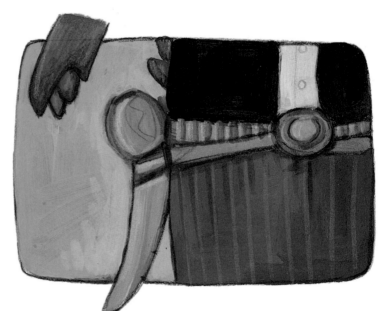

Pegleg Highnoon was the world's only pirate cowboy.

Among the cowboys, he was right famous-like for his ridin' and ropin'.

Among the pirates, he was legendary for his sailin' and swashbucklin'.

He wore a six-shooter on one hip and a cutlass on the other. And he was the only creature alive who spoke both Pirate and Cowboy.

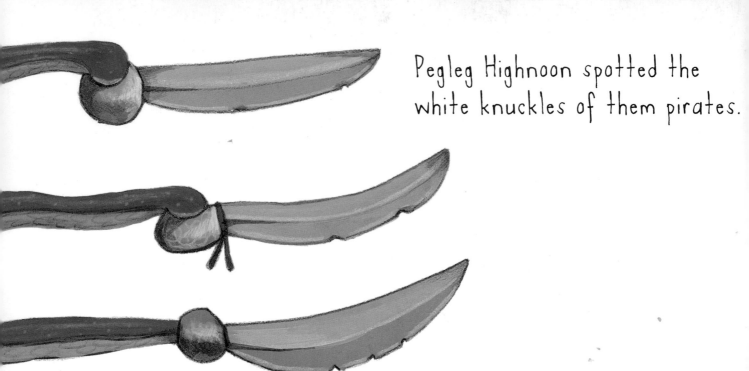

Pegleg Highnoon spotted the white knuckles of them pirates.

He spied the firmly planted boots of them cowboys.

And he knew that trouble was afoot.

And Pegleg Highnoon didn't like
anybody causing trouble . . .

. . . except Pegleg
Highnoon, that is.

Pegleg Highnoon rushed in, fixin' to teach a lesson to pirate and cowboy alike.

He was ready to root and toot.
He was prepared to swash and buckle.
His right hand reached for his pistol
and his left went for his sword.

But just then, the west wind shifted and he caught a foul
whiff coming off them cowboys. He turned his head away
and sniffed a nasty reek wafting from them pirates.

And forgetting the trouble that was afoot, thinking only of saving his own sense of smell, he grabbed his nose and turned to Black Bob McKraw.

"You and your posse smell worse than a polecat in an outhouse!"

he screeched in perfect Cowboy.

Then he rounded on Burnt Beard.

"You and your crew smell worse than three-day-old sunbaked shark bait!"

he bellowed in fluent Pirate.

"P-U! You guys stink!"

shouted Pegleg Highnoon,
waving a hanky in front
of his nose.

And that was
something they
both could
understand.

On that afternoon in the town of Old Cheyenne, Pegleg Highnoon did something that neither Black Bob McKraw nor Burnt Beard the Pirate had been able to do.

He found something that them pirates and them cowboys had in common.

Yes, it was their stench.
But it was a start.

Burnt Beard looked uneasily at Black Bob.
"We need a bath," he said, being sure to use
real small words.
Black Bob nodded. "So do we," he said.

So, leaving Pegleg Highnoon standing there holding his nose,

Black Bob McKraw led Burnt Beard the
Pirate to Old Cheyenne's one and only
bathhouse and saloon.

After a good soaping up, them
squeaky-clean cowboys poured
them pirates foaming mugs of
sarsaparilla. After a good drying
down, those well-swabbed pirates
shared the kegs of grog they'd
brought with them.

And the Old Cheyenne showdown between the pirates and the cowboys came to a peaceable—and sweet-smelling—end.

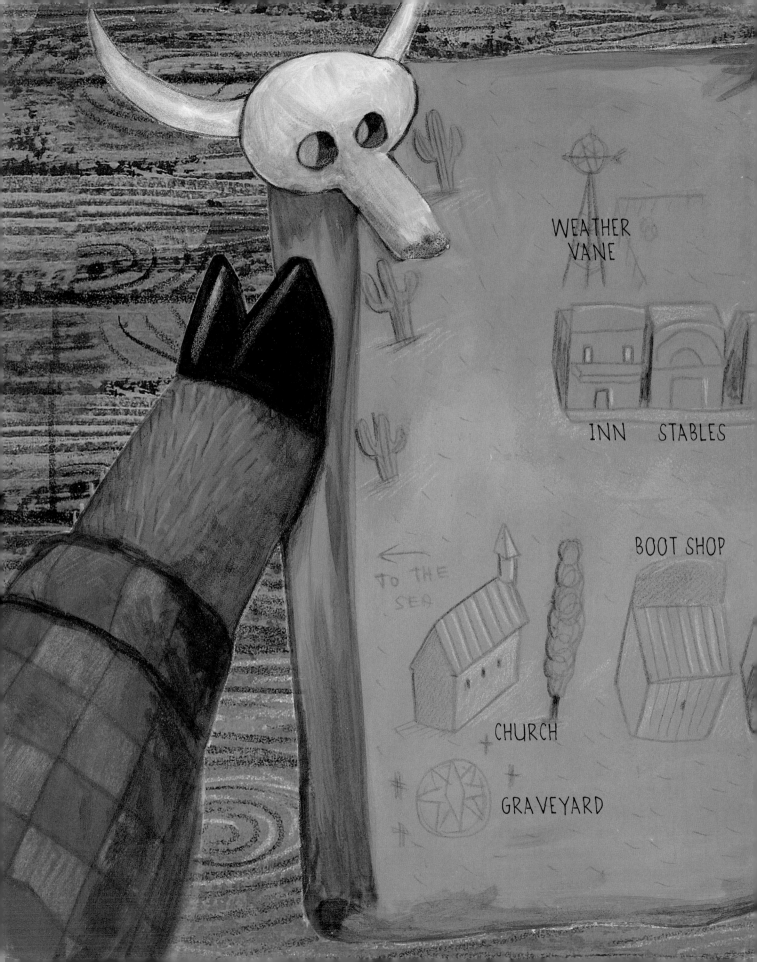